A Night in Santa's Great Big Bag

Kristin Kladstrup  Tim Jessell

VIKING

An Imprint of Penguin Group (USA) Inc.

VIKING
Published by Penguin Group
Penguin Young Readers Group, 345 Hudson Street, New York, New York 10014, U.S.A.
Penguin Group (Canada), 90 Eglinton Avenue East, Suite 700, Toronto, Ontario, Canada M4P 2Y3 (a division of Pearson Penguin Canada Inc.)
Penguin Books Ltd, 80 Strand, London WC2R 0RL, England
Penguin Ireland, 25 St Stephen's Green, Dublin 2, Ireland (a division of Penguin Books Ltd)
Penguin Group (Australia), 250 Camberwell Road, Camberwell, Victoria 3124, Australia (a division of Pearson Australia Group Pty Ltd)
Penguin Books India Pvt Ltd, 11 Community Centre, Panchsheel Park, New Delhi – 110 017, India
Penguin Group (NZ), 67 Apollo Drive, Rosedale, North Shore 0632, New Zealand (a division of Pearson New Zealand Ltd.)
Penguin Books (South Africa) (Pty) Ltd, 24 Sturdee Avenue, Rosebank, Johannesburg 2196, South Africa

Penguin Books Ltd, Registered Offices: 80 Strand, London WC2R 0RL, England

First published in 2010 by Viking, a division of Penguin Young Readers Group

1 3 5 7 9 10 8 6 4 2

Text copyright © Kristin Kladstrup, 2010
Illustrations copyright © Tim Jessell, 2010
All rights reserved

LIBRARY OF CONGRESS CATALOGING-IN-PUBLICATION DATA
Kladstrup, Kristin.
A night in Santa's great big bag / by Kristin Kladstrup ; illustrated by Tim Jessell.
p. cm.
Summary: Louis's favorite toy lamb inadvertently falls into Santa's bag on Christmas Eve.
ISBN 978-0-670-01165-0 (hardcover)
[1. Toys—Fiction. 2. Santa Claus—Fiction. 3. Christmas—Fiction.] I. Jessell, Tim, ill. II. Title.
PZ7.K6767Ni 2010
[E]—dc22
2009049440

Manufactured in China
Set in Cloister
Book design by Sam Kim

For John and Lambie —KK

For my mother and her devotion to all things Christmas,
and for my father: "Who do you think paid for it?" —TJ

"Tonight is Christmas Eve," Louis told Lamb. "Santa is coming with his great big bag. There are more toys inside it than in my toy box. There are more toys than in a toy store!"

Lamb, who happened to be Louis's favorite toy, liked toy boxes. He liked toy stores. That is why, when Louis was asleep, Lamb crept downstairs to watch Santa come down the chimney with his great big bag.

That is why, when Santa wasn't looking, Lamb tiptoed over to the bag.

He peeked in. It was dark, but he thought he could see a light in the distance. He pushed his nose in farther, and suddenly, Lamb was all the way inside the great big bag. He didn't even notice when Santa picked it up and went back out into the night.

Inside the bag, Lamb looked about in
wonder. It was so big that Lamb couldn't
see the end. All he could see were toys.
Balls bouncing!
Robots rumbling!
Helicopters hovering!
Trucks beeping!
Trains whistling!
If only Louis could see this, thought Lamb.

A doll with brown eyes and brown hair said to Lamb, "I am a Look-Alike Doll!" She sounded important, like Louis's older sister. "I am a present for a girl, and I look just like her," the doll told him. "Who do you look like?"

"I look like me," said Lamb. "Are all of these toys presents?"

"Of course," said the doll. "Whose present are you?"

Before Lamb could answer, a shout went up from the toys. "It's time! It's time!"

Santa's hand reached into the bag and picked up
a dump truck.

"Good-bye!" shouted the truck.

"Good-bye!" shouted the toys.

Santa's hand reached in again and picked up the doll.

"Good-bye!" said the doll.

"Good-bye!" shouted the toys.

"Where did they go?" said a voice near Lamb.

Turning around, Lamb saw a toy backhoe. The backhoe looked nervous, the way Louis had on the first day of school.

"That was Santa," said Lamb. "Louis says he gives presents to children on Christmas Eve."

"I'm supposed to be a present for a boy," said the backhoe.

"You will like that," said Lamb. "Santa brought Louis a toy backhoe last year. It can dig up rocks and sand."

"I have never dug up rocks and sand before," said the backhoe.

Lamb showed the backhoe how to use its bucket for digging and its shovel for pushing. "Sometimes Louis lets me ride in the shovel," Lamb said.

Lamb climbed in, and the backhoe took him on a ride through Santa's bag.

Some of the toys they met didn't know what to expect when
Santa delivered them.

A jigsaw puzzle said, "I used to be a picture of a puppy.
Now I'm all broken into pieces."

Lamb said, "Don't worry! Someone will put you back
together. That's what Louis does with jigsaw puzzles."

A train engine was having trouble pulling its cars along a wooden track. "I can't get them to follow me!" it wailed.

"That happens to Louis's train engine sometimes," said Lamb. "You are backward. You need to go to the other end of the cars."

Lamb liked talking to the toys. He liked making them feel better. "Good-bye!" he called as, one by one, they left the great big bag.

"Good-bye!" called the backhoe, when it was its turn to go.
"I hope my boy has a lamb just like you!"

Now there were only two toys left in the great big bag: Lamb and a little bunny. The bunny's eyes were squeezed shut.

"What are you doing?" asked Lamb.

"Santa is giving me to a little girl," said the bunny. "I am supposed to go to sleep with her every night. So I am practicing."

Lamb giggled. "You don't need to practice going to sleep!"

"No?" The bunny opened his eyes.

"Louis and I just crawl under the covers and talk to each other until we fall asleep," said Lamb. "It's the easiest thing in the world."

Then Santa took the bunny out of the bag, and Lamb was alone. He couldn't help thinking of Louis. He wished he were home, under the covers with him. And then Lamb had a terrible thought: What if Santa mistook him for a present? What if he gave him to somebody else? Somebody who wasn't Louis!

Oh, dear! Here was Santa's hand, coming to get him!

A moment later Lamb was out of the bag. The air was cold and Santa was looking down at him. "Why, Lamb," said Santa. "What are you doing in my bag?"

"I wanted to see the toys!" cried Lamb. "I'm not a present! I belong to Louis!"

"Well, I know that," said Santa. "I brought you to Louis when he was only a baby. Don't you remember?"

Lamb did not.

"I suppose you were too young," said Santa. "Just a baby yourself."

"Please don't give me to somebody else!" said Lamb.

"Now why would I do that?" said Santa. "I am going to take you back home to Louis!"

And that is how Lamb came to sit beside Santa in his sleigh.
There were stars above him. There were stars below him too.
Santa said these stars were houses with lights.

One of those houses belonged to Louis, and Lamb thought he remembered, just a little, coming to that house a long time ago.

"Louis isn't very good at remembering things from when he was a baby either," said Lamb as Santa tucked him into Louis's stocking.

"Do you think he will remember that this is where he found you the first time?" asked Santa.

"I will tell him," said Lamb. "I will tell him all about your great big bag!"

And on Christmas morning, that is exactly what Lamb did.